ZOOM UPSTREAM

For Montezuma — Zoom himself 1975-1986. — TW-J

For Alberta and her Guy. — EB

A Groundwood Book
Douglas & McIntyre
585 Bloor Street West
Toronto, Ontario M6G 1K5

Canadian Cataloguing in Publication Data

Wynne-Jones, Tim
Zoom upstream

ISBN 0-88899-109-6

1. Cats — Juvenile fiction. I. Beddows, Eric,
1951- . II. Title.

PS8595.Y44Z6 1992   jC813'.54   C92-094419-1

PZ7.W947o 1992

Design by Michael Solomon
Printed and bound in Hong Kong
by Everbest Printing Co., Ltd.

ZOOM UPSTREAM

BY
Tim Wynne-Jones

PICTURES BY
Eric Beddows

A GROUNDWOOD BOOK
Douglas & McIntyre
TORONTO/VANCOUVER

It was fall. Zoom was visiting his friend Maria. They were in her back garden, raking leaves and planting lily bulbs for spring. Zoom pruned the roses with his very own pruning shears.

The sun was warm. Zoom stretched out on a lawn chair by the goldfish pond for a snooze.

The telephone rang.

"I'll get it," said Maria.

Zoom woke up feeling chilly. The sky had clouded over. Maria was not there. Zoom followed her muddy boot prints to the kitchen.

She had left him a hastily scribbled note.

"It's the captain. Had to go. No time to lose!"

"Uncle Roy!" thought Zoom. "What trouble is he in now?"

Zoom followed Maria's footsteps to the library.
They ended at a bookcase. There was a light coming
from a space on the shelf where a book had been.
It lay on the table.

Zoom climbed up onto the book and looked into
the bookcase.

"This must be the way," he said.

At the back of the bookshelf a flight of stairs spiraled down into darkness. The stairway was made entirely of books!

Down and down the stairway curled. Zoom was a little bit frightened. Then he heard something that cheered him up — the sound of water lapping against stone.

Zoom found himself on a levee by a dark river. There were old crates piled everywhere, dusty and cobwebby. He chose an empty one his size, found a stick for a paddle, and pushed himself out onto the water.

"If there's trouble," thought Zoom, "Maria might need some help."

Zoom dipped his paddle into the oily waters. The current pulled him along the river's winding course. The air grew warmer.

"Brrrp! Brrrp!"

He heard something croaking.

Swooooosh!

Bats!

He saw a log. A log with eyes.

Then Zoom's crate began to spin, around and around, caught in the rapids, pulling him faster and faster.

Whoooosh!

Zoom closed his eyes and hung on tight.

Thump!

He banged into a stone dock.

He wasn't hurt. Carefully he climbed from his crate into a room aglow with torches. The walls were crawling with pictures, and all the pictures were of cats. There were cats on the ceiling, cats carved out of stone, their eyes twinkling jewels. And everywhere around him there were cloth-covered catlike shapes.

"Mummies," thought Zoom. "This must be Egypt!"

He had always wanted to go to Egypt. But where was the desert? Where were the pyramids? And most of all, where was the mighty Nile? The dark little river seemed to end at this room.

Boom! Boom! Boom!

Drums. Someone was coming.

Zoom froze. At the end of the room two enormous stone cats stood sentinel on either side of a huge stone slab. As Zoom watched, one of the stone cats raised its paw. Slowly.

Then there was a loud creaking and rumbling. The slab creaked open. A procession marched into the room – cats in hats bearing a mummy on a litter.

"Bisso, Bubastis, Bastet," chanted the cat with the tallest hat.

"Bisso, Bubastis, Bastet," the other cats answered. They placed the mummy on the floor, and then –

Boom! Boom! Boom!

They were gone, just like that. The slab closed after them.

Thud.

"Phew! That was close," whispered Zoom.

He looked at the new mummy. It was much bigger than the other mummies and the shape looked awfully familiar. Zoom felt queasy inside. Then the mummy moved.

"Get me out of here," cried a muffled but very familiar voice.

"Don't worry," said Zoom. "I'll get you out."

His pruning shears were in his coat pocket!

It didn't take him long to cut the mummy open. Maria!

"Am I glad to see you!" she said.

Maria gave Zoom a big hug. Then she began to snoop around the room. Zoom's heart sank. "Are you looking for Uncle Roy?" he asked.

"That's right," said Maria.

Zoom stared into the gloom. None of the mummies moved.

"I guess we're too late," he mumbled. Maria did not hear him.

"Aha!" she said, picking up something shiny from the cold stone floor. A silver button.

Zoom recognized it right away. "It's from Uncle Roy's captain's uniform," he said with dismay.

"Right again," said Maria.

Zoom had never felt so sad in his life. "I wonder which mummy he is?" he said.

To his surprise, Maria laughed. "Captain Roy, a mummy? I doubt it!"

"You mean," said Zoom, "he got away?"

Maria nodded. "And he left us a clue," she said, holding up the button.

Zoom jumped for joy.

"We're on the right track," said Maria. "Now if we could just get out of this catacomb."

"I think I know the way," said Zoom.

He walked to the end of the room, to the stone sentinel cats. He pushed on the cat's paw with all his might. Finally, there was a loud creaking and rumbling. The slab opened.

"Yahoo!" cried Maria.

"Where now?" asked Zoom.

"Look for buttons," said Maria.

They found themselves in a cavernous hallway lined with towering, glowering cats, whose eyes followed them as they hurried along. Zoom tried to keep his own eyes on the ground.

Boom! Boom! Boom!

The sound of the drums echoed off the walls. Were they behind or up ahead? Zoom couldn't tell.

Then he saw silver. The second button. Maria found the third.

Boom! Boom! Boom!

Were the drums getting closer?

Left, then right, Zoom and Maria followed the clues. Four, five, six, seven – ah!

Suddenly they burst out of the murky tomb onto a pier under a gentle Egyptian night. A rowboat awaited them, something silver on the seat glinting in the starlight.

"The last button," said Maria as she and Zoom clambered on board. Maria took up the oars. Zoom made his way to the bow. Far ahead he could see a clipper sitting under a crescent moon.

"The Catship!" he cried.

The rowboat sped out onto the wide black river. The mighty Nile. Zoom watched as the Catship loomed nearer and nearer. He heard a concertina and someone singing.

Then –

"Ahoy! Hurrah! Halloo!"

And there was the dark side of the ship and a rope ladder and, reaching down with a smile on his face, a large yellow tomcat in a captain's hat.

Uncle Roy.

"Welcome aboard," he said. "And just in time for a bowl of grog."

Zoom couldn't speak for smiling.

"We've got quite the trip ahead of us," said Roy.

"Where to?" asked Zoom.

"Upstream," said Captain Roy. "To search for the source of the Nile. Are you game, my small friend?"

"Yes," said Zoom.

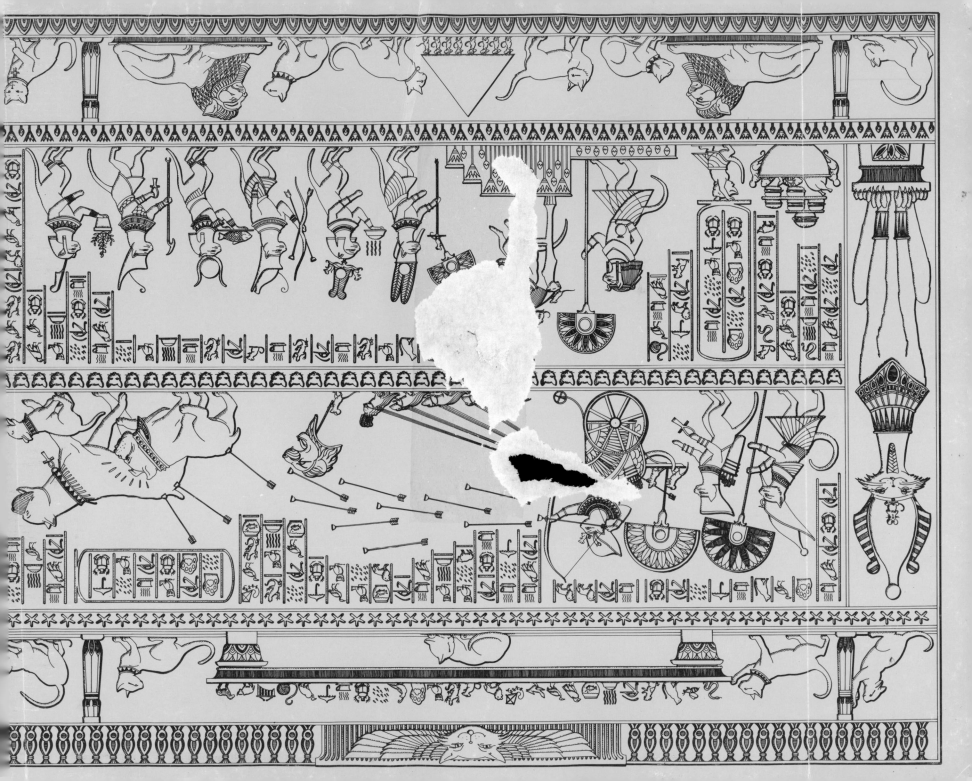